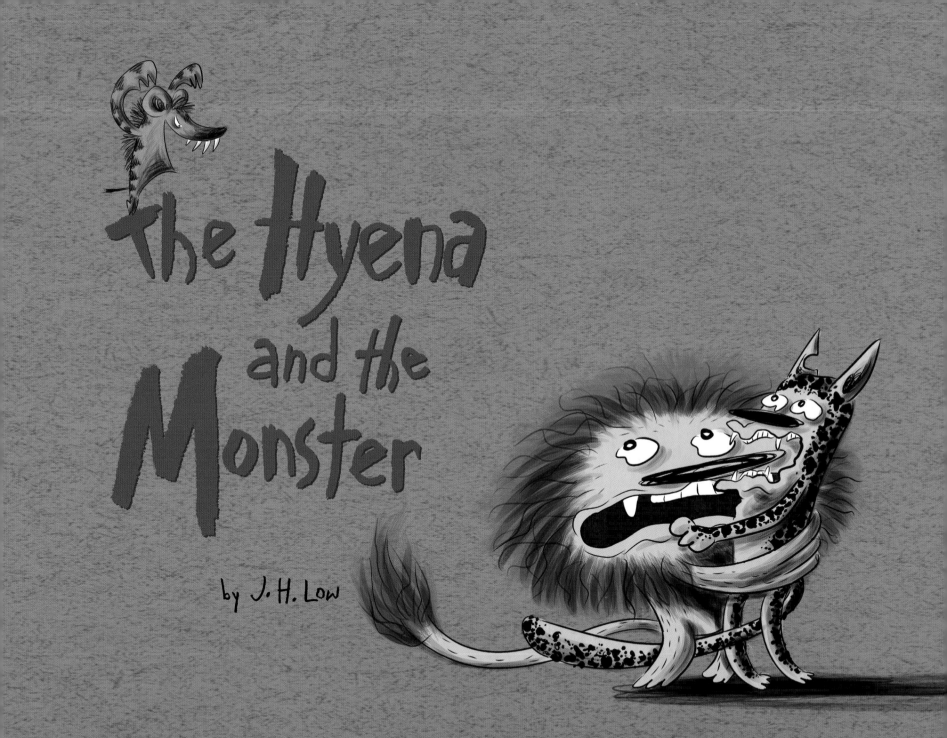

The Hyena and the Monster

by J. H. Low

Marshall Cavendish
Children

© 2016 Marshall Cavendish International (Asia) Private Limited

Published by Marshall Cavendish Children
An imprint of Marshall Cavendish International

First published in Chinese by Marshall Cavendish Education, 2012

Other Marshall Cavendish Offices:
Marshall Cavendish Corporation. 99 White Plains Road, Tarrytown NY 10591-9001, USA • Marshall Cavendish International (Thailand) Co Ltd. 253 Asoke, 12th Flr, Sukhumvit 21 Road, Klongtoey Nua, Wattana, Bangkok 10110, Thailand • Marshall Cavendish (Malaysia) Sdn Bhd, Times Subang, Lot 46, Subang Hi-Tech Industrial Park, Batu Tiga, 40000 Shah Alam, Selangor Darul Ehsan, Malaysia.

Marshall Cavendish is a trademark of Times Publishing Limited

National Library Board, Singapore Cataloguing-in-Publication Data

Low, Joo Hong, author.
The hyena and the monster / by J.H. Low. – Singapore : Marshall Cavendish Children, 2015.
pages cm. – (Four Tooth and friends)
ISBN : 978-981-4721-69-1

1. Friendship – Juvenile fiction. 2. Animals – Juvenile fiction. I. Title.
II. Series: Four Tooth and friends.

PZ7
428.6 -- dc23   OCN920358204

Printed by Times Offset (M) Sdn Bhd

About this Book

The Hyena and the Monster is inspired by the Chinese idiom, 狐假虎威 (hu jia hu wei), about the story of a quick-witted fox.

One day, a fox was caught by a tiger and was about to be eaten when he came up with a plan. He pretended to be outraged to be so badly treated by the tiger, saying that he was king over all the animals and that the tiger would be severely punished if he caused him any harm. To prove his point, he told the tiger to take a walk with him through the jungle. During the walk, all the animals fled in fear when they saw the pair. Seeing this, the tiger was convinced that the fox was truly king and let him go.

This idiom is often used to describe people who bully others by boasting of their powerful connections.

The Hyena and the Monster gives an interesting twist to this idiom, and teaches young readers essential lessons about friendship. This entertaining story, filled with wit and humour, will enthral readers of all ages.

It was late at night and
Four Tooth the hyena was fast asleep.
Suddenly, a deafening sound jolted him!
It seemed to come from the jungle.

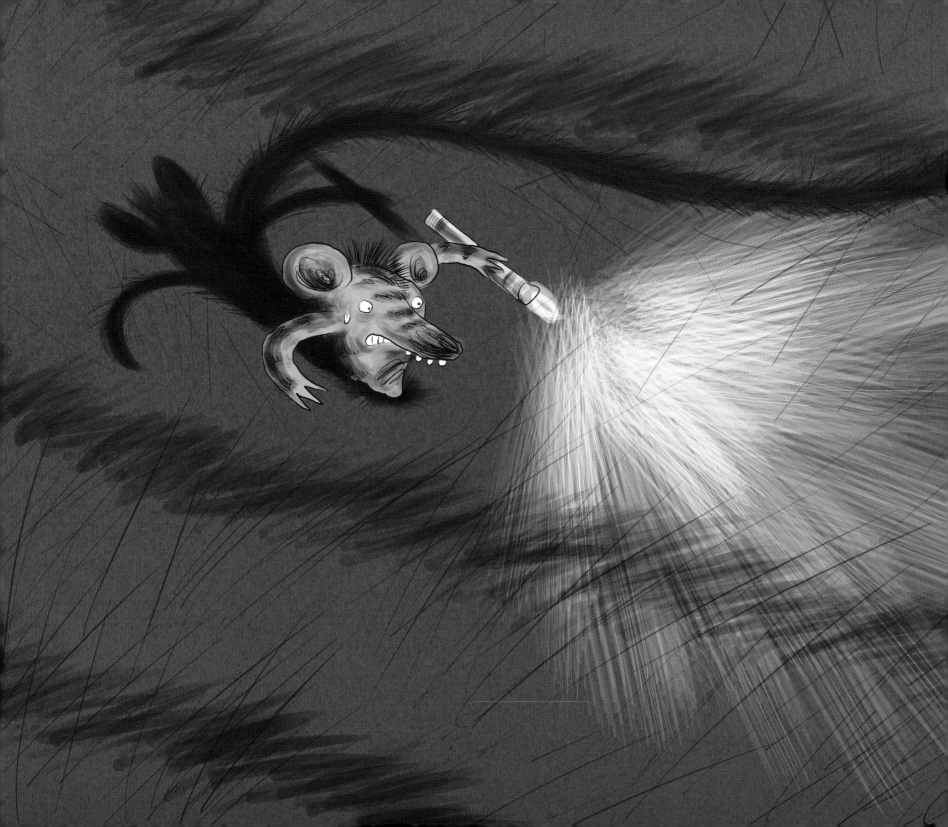

What could it be?
Four Tooth decided to investigate.
It was a long walk to the jungle,
and it was very dark.
But Four Tooth was brave.

In the jungle, what Four Tooth saw gave him a fright!

Where there were trees, there were now only stumps.
What was happening?

Coarse
black hair

Long
claw
marks

Four Tooth was curious.
He decided to investigate.
He found many clues.

An enormous
footprint

"A monster!" concluded Four Tooth.
"I must warn the others!"

Crime Scene

But the animals laughed at Four Tooth.
"Monsters don't exist!" they chuckled.

Beware the monster!

That made Four Tooth very angry.
He vowed to teach them a lesson!

He hunted **HIGH**

and he hunted
LOW

until he found everything he needed

to make a **MONSTER** costume!

"This will teach them not to laugh at me!"

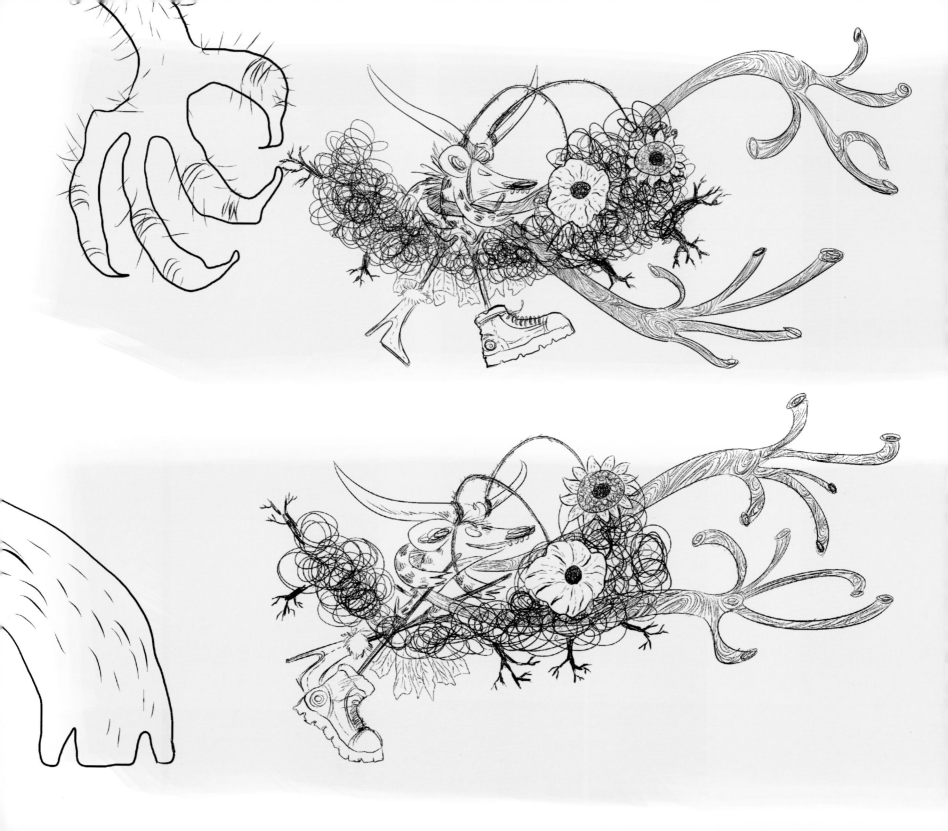

He put on his monster costume to frighten the little animals.

And the little animals ran away!

He put on his monster costume to frighten Chip Ear.

And Chip Ear ran away!

He put on his monster costume to frighten all the animals.

And all the animals ran away!

Four Tooth was happy that he had
taught the animals a lesson.
Then he noticed that he wasn't alone.

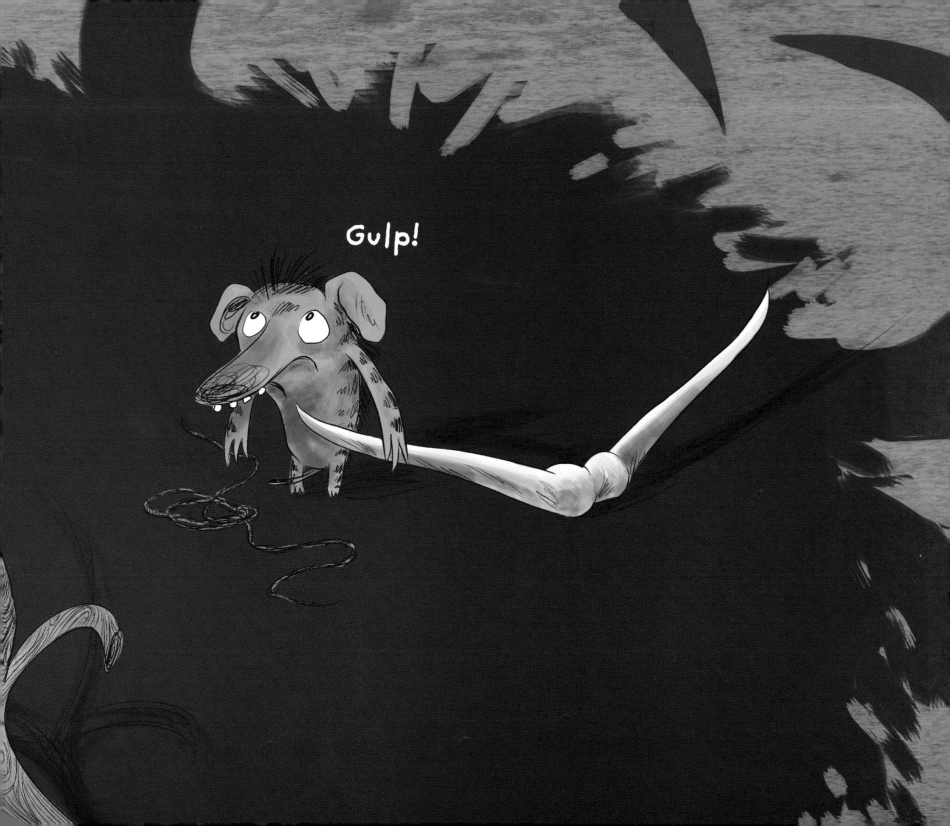

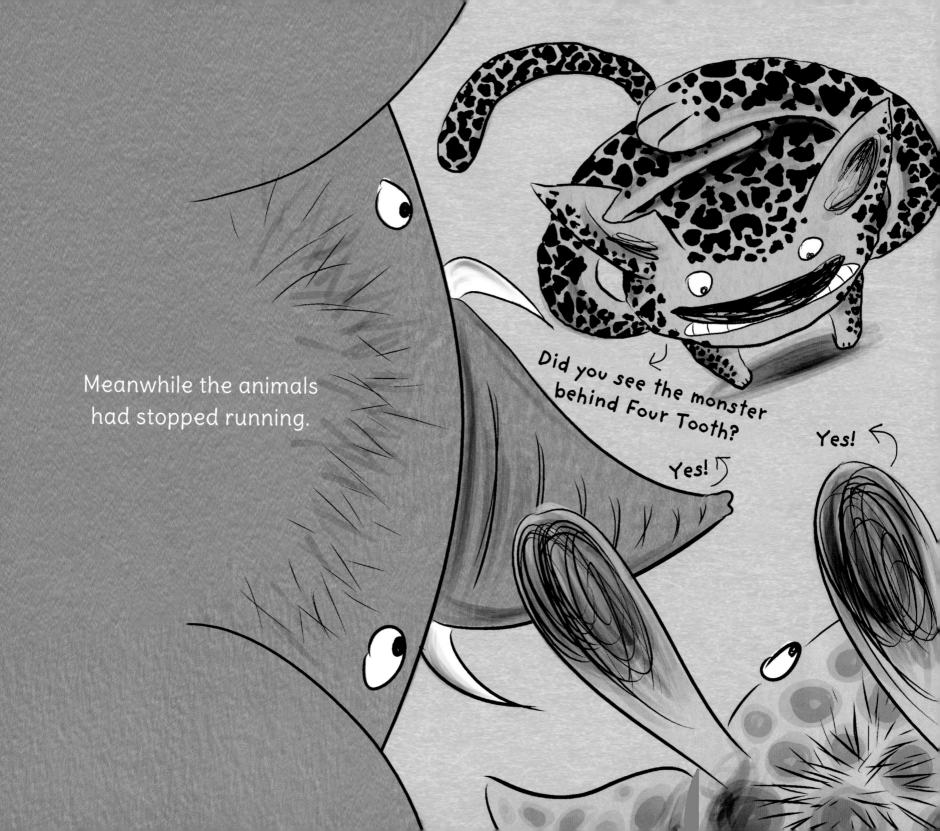

Meanwhile the animals had stopped running.

Did you see the monster behind Four Tooth?

Yes!

Yes!

Four Tooth was in the claws of the monster!
Although they were very afraid,
the animals went up to the monster
and begged him to let Four Tooth go.

Four Tooth
is our friend.
Please let him go.

Touched by their love for Four Tooth,
the monster let Four Tooth go.

Trees taste
so much better
than hyenas!

About the Author and Illustrator

J.H. Low has always been a passionate artist, illustrator and
creator of stories. He holds a BA (Honours) in Fine Arts from the
University of Leeds, UK, and a MA in Children's Books Illustration from
the Anglia Ruskin University, UK. In 2009, he received the prestigious
Macmillan Prize for Children's Picture Book Illustration for
There Is Nothing Buried Here, which was translated into
Chinese and became his first published book.

J.H.'s illustrations are spontaneous and masterful, and often imbued with
a light touch of humour. He is the illustrator of *Dragon's Egg* (2012) by
award-winning author, Carolyn Goodwin. He is also the author and illustrator
of the much-loved children's book, *Lost in the Gardens* (2015),
the first in a series of books on Singapore's attractions.